For Jermaine ~ T.C.

For my Nan ~ P.H.

First published 2003 by Walker Books Ltd
87 Vauxhall Walk, London SE11 5HJ

This edition published 2004

10 9 8 7 6 5 4 3 2

Text © 2003 Trish Cooke
Illustrations © 2003 Paul Howard

The right of Trish Cooke and Paul Howard
to be identified as author and illustrator respectively
of this work has been asserted by them in accordance
with the Copyright, Designs and Patents Act 1988

This book has been typeset in Block Regular

Printed in China

British Library Cataloguing in Publication Data:
a catalogue record for this book is available
from the British Library

ISBN 1-84428-782-3

www.walkerbooks.co.uk

Full, Full, Full of LOVE

Trish Cooke

illustrated by

Paul Howard

WALKER BOOKS
AND SUBSIDIARIES

LONDON • BOSTON • SYDNEY • AUCKLAND

On Sunday, Mum took Jay Jay
to Grannie's house.
"I'll go get Dad," Mum said.
"I won't be long!"

Gran is soft and warm and full,
full of hugs and kisses.
Kiss, kiss.
Hugs and cuddles.

Grannie was cooking.

The dinner smelled lovely.

"Is dinner ready, Gran?" asked Jay Jay.

But Gran shook her head.

"Dinner's not ready yet," she said.

"Come… Let's put out the dishes."

Grannie's cupboard is always full,
full of colourful dishes.

Clink, clank.

Clatter, clatter.

But Jay Jay was hungry.

"Is dinner ready now?" he asked.

Gran shook her head.

"Dinner's not ready yet," she said.

"Come... Let's feed the fish."

Grannie's fish tank is full,

full of all kinds of fishes.

Splash, splish.

Wiggle, wiggle.

But Jay Jay was hungry.

So Jay Jay asked again,

"Is dinner ready NOW, Gran?"

Gran shook her head.

"Dinner's not ready yet," she said.

"Come... Let's ..."

Then Jay Jay saw the sweety tin.

Grannie's sweety tin was full,

full up to the brim.

Tip, tip.

Struggle, juggle.

Gran said, "No!"
But seeing those sweets
had made Jay Jay even hungrier
than before.
So he asked again,
"Is dinner NEARLY ready, Gran?"
Gran shook her head.
"Dinner's not ready yet," she said.
"Come, let's look for the others."

So they looked out of the window
and they waited, and waited.
Tick, tock.
Snuggle, cuddle.

Then Jay Jay saw a car come round
the corner, then another,
and another,

and the cars stopped
one behind the other.
And out they all came.

Uncles and aunties, cousins and friends,
Mummy and Daddy.
All come for Sunday dinner at Grannie's!

"Dinner MUST be ready now, Gran!"
Jay Jay grinned. And Gran laughed.
"*Mmmmmmmmmm, I think it is!*"

There were
runner-beans,
peas and yams,
macaroni cheese,
potatoes
and ham.

Dumplings,
chicken,
collard greens,
pasta salad,
rice and red beans!
There was apple pie
and vanilla ice cream,
fresh peach cobbler covered in steam,
raspberry sauce,
coffee and tea –
plenty, plenty for
everybody!

Jay Jay said, "I'm going to pop!"
And Cousin said, "I have to stop!"
"More pie please!" Uncle said,
and Auntie and Mum shook their heads.
"Not for me."
"I've had enough!"
Grannie let out a big belly laugh.
Dad said, "Just a little bit more!"
and on top of his ice cream
Gran started to pour
some more
raspberry sauce.

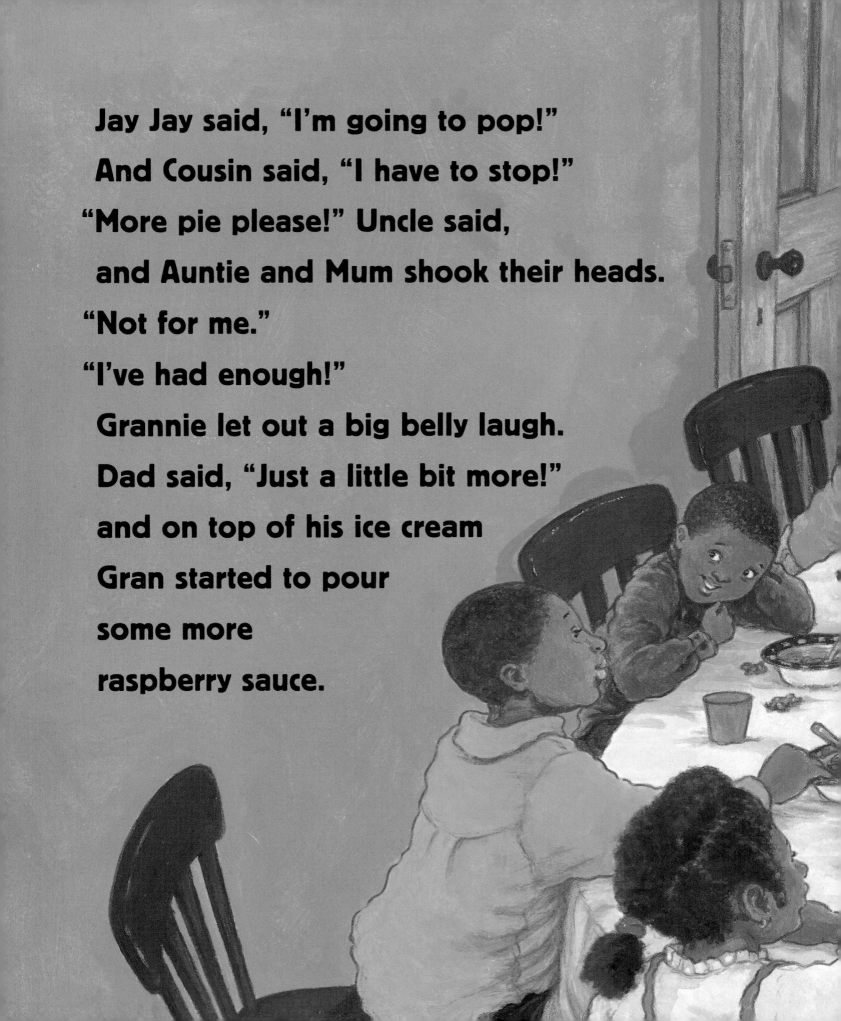

Everybody was full,
full of Grannie's dinner!
Yum, yum.
Giggle, giggle.

Then Grannie pulled up a stool,
put up her feet
and sighed.

"One wash, one dry!"

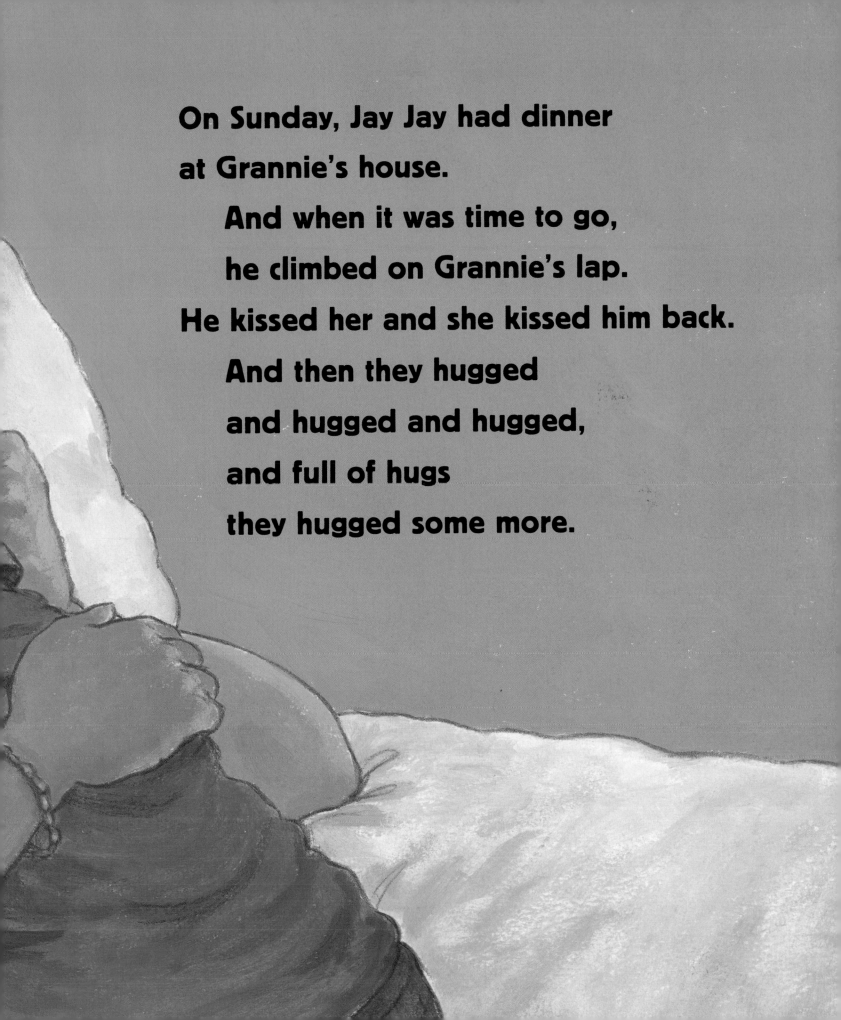

On Sunday, Jay Jay had dinner
at Grannie's house.
　　And when it was time to go,
　　he climbed on Grannie's lap.
He kissed her and she kissed him back.
　　And then they hugged
　　and hugged and hugged,
　　and full of hugs
　　they hugged some more.

Grannie's house is always full,

  full of hugs and kisses,

  full of tasty dishes,

  full of all kinds of fishes,

  full to the brim with happy faces,

  full, full, full of love.

That's Sunday dinner at Grannie's house!